Easter Bunny
Are You for Real?

Written By **Harold Myra**

Illustrated by **Dwight Walles**

THOMAS NELSON PUBLISHERS
Nashville

For
Gregory David Myra

Published in Nashville, Tennessee, by Thomas Nelson, Inc. and distributed in Canada by Lawson Falle, Ltd., Cambridge, Ontario.

Printed in the United States of America.

Scripture quotation on page 27 from the King James Version of the Bible.

Scripture quotation on page 28 from *The Living Bible* (Wheaton, Ill.: Tyndale House Publishers, 1971) and used by permission.

ISBN 0-8407-5148-6
Library of Congress catalog number: 78-21268

7 8 9 10 - 90 89 88 87

Michelle ran into the garage. "Hey Dad! It's okay with you if we make the ear here, right?"

"The ear?" her father asked.

"The bunny ear! See," she explained, showing him a frame three feet tall. "I offered our garage."

Michelle described the huge papier mache Easter bunny her school was making. "Everybody's helping! Our class does the ears. And the kindergartners get to ride it!"

"Ride it?"

"They climb all over it at the top of the hill. It'll be stuffed with eggs and jelly beans and it'll break like a Mexican piñata at Christmas!"

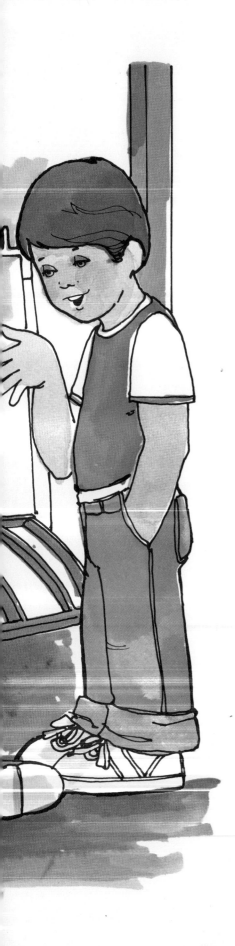

From then on, each time Dad entered the garage, he bumped into kids dipping paper into water and flour or mixing another color, saying things like "No, no, *that's* not how she said to do it," or "You're supposed to *smear* it."

Michelle's brother Todd watched, unimpressed. "Looks like a pretty wobbly ear to me."

"Rabbit ears are supposed to be floppy," Michelle answered.

"Where'd you find all those dumb colors?"

"They're Easter colors!"

Early Saturday morning the whole family went to school. Fathers and teachers put feet and legs and ears and face and arms all together. The result was . . . well, a strange looking rabbit.

His vest turned out grass green, but with purple and red rivers running through it. Michelle and her class had made ears which looked as if giant orange, cherry, lemon, and grape Life Savers had all melted over them and then someone had sprayed on blobs of shaving cream. The face was bright purple with a giant grin. Altogether, Oswald—which is what the kids named him—was probably the most unusual patchwork bunny ever made. He would stand guarding the school until the big event that evening.

Daddy lifted little Greg to his shoulders. "Isn't Oswald a huge Easter bunny, Greg?"

"And a *funny* bunny?" Mommy asked.

"No!" Greg declared. "That Easter bunny is naughty!"

"Now *where* did you hear that?" Daddy asked, smiling.

"That's a naughty Easter bunny," Greg repeated very seriously, nodding his head up and down. *"Naughty!"*

Greg was too young to explain himself, so after they got home, Daddy asked Michelle and Todd, "Say, where'd Greg get this 'naughty Easter bunny' idea?"

Michelle and Todd thought awhile. Finally Michelle said, "I remember someone at church saying it's a shame the way kids get all excited about the Easter bunny."

"Why shouldn't we get excited about the Easter bunny?" Todd asked. "Michelle's Oswald is crazy. But I love those chocolate ones you can eat all up."

"But, Todd," his sister lectured, "what *does* the Easter bunny have to do with Easter? They never talk about him in Sunday school." There was a pause. "Daddy, how'd the Easter bunny get into Easter anyhow?"

"Well," said Daddy, sitting down with the kids, "let's go back to the beginning . . . back to Jesus' friends just before the first Easter. They had seen Jesus grabbed by soldiers. They saw Him killed on the cross, then buried. All their dreams were gone. What a terrible day! Jesus was dead.

"But three days later—that first Easter dawn—Jesus broke out of His grave. He was alive again! He walked and talked with His friends. He ate with them. 'See my hands and my feet,' Jesus told them. 'It is I. Touch me and see!'"*

12   *Luke 24:39.

"His disciples suddenly knew everything was different. Jesus would live
forever. *And they would, too!* Now
they knew death was the beginning,
not the end."

13

"But why did Jesus let those bad guys kill Him in the first place?" Todd asked. "Especially if He was so powerful, like superman . . .?"

"Jesus could have destroyed them. But they were people He had come to save. All of us are 'bad guys,' you know—we've all disobeyed God. But Jesus died and rose again so God could forgive us—so we could live forever with Him."

"But where'd the Easter bunny come in?" Michelle interrupted.

"While the early Christians celebrated Easter, others were celebrating springtime. After a cold, dark winter, the people were glad to see new leaves and flowers, and animals having babies—kittens and chicks and foals—and, yes, bunnies. Rabbit stories just grew out of that. Like the old story from Germany in which a poor woman put colored eggs in a nest. Just as her children discovered them, a rabbit leaped away. Soon kids said that the rabbit had brought the eggs. Even today, they're making up new TV stories about the Easter bunny."

"You mean," asked Michelle, "the Easter bunny has *nothing* to do with the real Easter?"

"That's right. He's part of celebrating spring— but that's all. Spring is nature coming back to life again—it's God's

picture of Jesus rising from the dead. But most people don't think of that."

"Where'd the eggs come in?" Mother called from the kitchen as she spooned hard boiled eggs out of a pot. Soon all three kids had scrambled to the kitchen table and were picking favorite colors.

"During Lent, in very ancient times, Christians didn't eat eggs," Daddy began. "What's Lent?" interrupted Todd as he dunked a half-red egg into the cup of purple dye.

"A fast—which means not eating . . ."

"Isn't that kinda dumb?" Todd asked.

"No. Christ fasted. Lent is a time when we can remember the sufferings of Jesus and ask forgiveness for our sins. It reminds us of dying with Christ. Then comes Easter—the sad time is over. Feast time arrives! Eggs made people think of new life. They were brought to the table colored red for Easter joy. We have new life in Christ, so eat and make merry!"

"I like that part," Todd observed.

"There are lots of customs with eggs," Daddy continued. "For instance, Christians in Greece and Romania tap their red eggs together as an Easter greeting. One person says, 'Christ is risen.' The other replies, 'He is risen, indeed!'"

"I'm getting mixed up," Michelle objected, "I don't remember eggs in the Bible stories."

"You're right, Michelle. Oh, some say Mary used to amuse baby Jesus by boiling eggs and coloring them. But that's just a story. The confusion comes because the real Easter and all this springtime merriment got mixed together over the centuries. For hundreds of years people have been hiding eggs and telling stories of how the Easter bunny burns wild flowers to make dye."

"Is that okay—to celebrate spring like that?" asked Michelle.

"Sure—if we also remember the real Easter. God wants us to celebrate His world—chicks, bunnies, eggs—He made them all. But Easter is the day God's Son rose from the dead! How does God feel if we only talk about new clothes and parades and bunnies?"

After supper, and lots more talk, it was time for the big event at school. At least two hundred children surrounded Oswald while about twenty-five smaller kids waited for the signal to climb up and ride.

The whistle blew. Todd grabbed for Oswald's knee and pulled himself up. Other kids took running leaps, grabbing anywhere and pulling themselves up. Soon they were on Oswald's back, up on his head, hanging onto his vest. Kids' feet and knees and arms broke through. Suddenly all of Oswald was crashing and rolling down the hill, with little kids jumping and falling off with cheers and laughter, and little fingers grabbing for jelly beans and candy eggs.

A second whistle blew. As eggs rolled, the bigger kids ran after them, grabbing, laughing, shouting, tripping.

Todd proudly brought twelve jelly beans and two eggs to the car. Michelle started sharing her loot with Greg. She was having a wonderful time—but she was also worried about what God might be thinking.

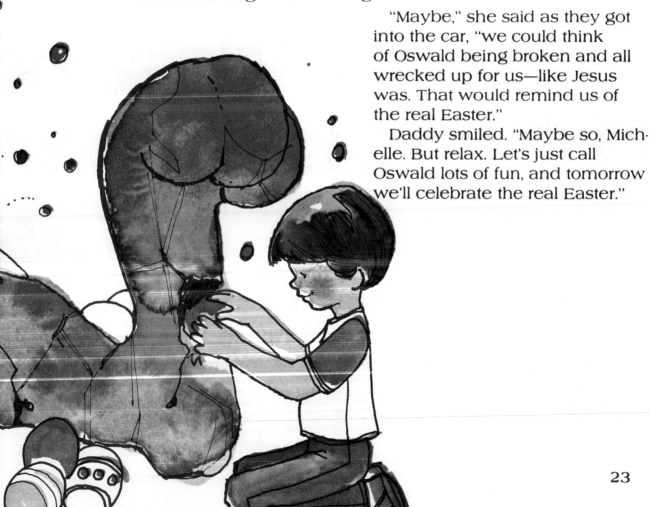

"Maybe," she said as they got into the car, "we could think of Oswald being broken and all wrecked up for us—like Jesus was. That would remind us of the real Easter."

Daddy smiled. "Maybe so, Michelle. But relax. Let's just call Oswald lots of fun, and tomorrow we'll celebrate the real Easter."

23

The next morning *very* early, while it was
still dark, three children and two parents
went sleepily to the patio to wait for
the Easter sunrise. Slowly, slowly, a bit of pink
light began on the horizon. It seemed a very
long time before they saw the edge of the sun.
It spread its rays everywhere into the dark
world.

Daddy whispered, "Some used to say the
sun actually skipped for joy every Easter
morning, and if you got up, you'd see it."

"I *love* the Easter-rise," stated Greg
solemnly. Daddy and Mommy smiled.

"It's kind of like Narnia,* isn't it, Dad?" Michelle asked, looking at the half-risen sun.

"Oh?"

"Like the last book when the children get killed in a railway accident, but they go higher and higher into those new worlds, and they see the One who died and all their old friends . . ."

26

They all sat and watched as the sun took over the entire sky. Daddy noticed a serious look on Michelle's face. He could tell she was thinking of someone she knew who had died not long ago.

Finally Michelle said, "Death is kind of like having a friend in Norway or something."

"Oh?"

"She's alive. Eventually I'll see her again. I mean, she's not really *dead*. She's just alive somewhere else."

"That's true. And it's all because God loves us so much," Mother added. "Let's say John 3:16 together: *'For God so loved the world that he gave his only begotten Son, that whosoever believeth in him should not perish, but have everlasting life.'*"

Later that morning, they sat in church and heard the choir sing:

> *'Up from the grave he arose,*
> *With a mighty triumph o'er his foes.'*

The sound of all the strong voices rushed through them like cheers at a ball game. Then someone read from the Bible: "But I am telling you this strange and wonderful secret: we shall all be given new bodies! It will all happen in a moment, in the twinkling of an eye. . . . For there will be a trumpet blast from the sky and all the Christians who have died will suddenly become alive, with new bodies that will never, never die."*

"You know," Daddy told them on the way home, "Easter is the oldest Christian festival. To the early church, Jesus' rising from the dead was so important it was a *weekly* celebration. Every Sunday was Easter Sunday."

*From 1 Corinthians 1:51-2, *The Living Bible*.

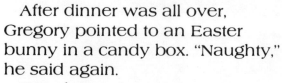

After dinner was all over, Gregory pointed to an Easter bunny in a candy box. "Naughty," he said again.

"You know, in some ways Greg's right," Michelle declared. "It's almost as if the Easter bunny *tries* to get people to forget the real Easter. That's crazy!"

30

"My favorite way of thinking about the Easter bunny," Daddy said, "is that a rabbit spends the winter in a dark hole in the earth. Kind of like the burial of Jesus. But then, picture a rabbit leaping out of that hole in the springtime, jumping and skipping in the sunlight, free and full of life! That's how we've been set free by our risen Lord Jesus."

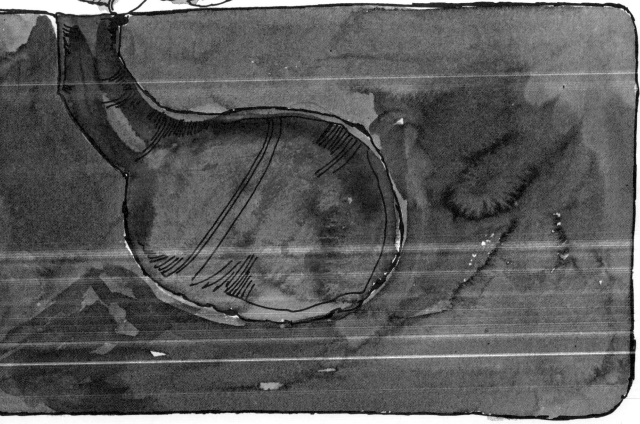

By this time. Greg was munching the ears off his "naughty" rabbit.

"Well," Todd said, "one good thing about the Easter bunny—he sure got us talking a lot about God and Easter and everything this year."

"Yes," Daddy agreed, "and since God made both rabbits and chocolate, I think I'll have a little bite . . . "

And he did.